The
Moon
Jumpers

Summer night is the cool dark grass
And big tired trees
With the moon sailing
On a wind.

THE

THE MOON JUMPERS

Printed in the United States of America

Text copyright © 1959 by Janice May Udry

Pictures copyright © 1959 by Maurice Sendak

All rights in this book are reserved.

Standard Book Number 978-0-06-028460-2 (Trade Edition)

HarperCollins Publishers, New York, NY 10022

12 13 14 15 16   LP   10 9 8 7 6 5 4 3 2 1

MOON JUMPERS

by JANICE MAY UDRY

pictures by MAURICE SENDAK

HARPER COLLINS

The sun is tired. It goes down the sky into the drowsy hills.

The sunflowers lean. They fall asleep to dream of tomorrow's sun.

The moon is up! Now the owl is awake in the pine tree. The cat steps out and walks around the edge of the garden and then goes out the gate.

Beyond the gate the road winds into darkness.

The cool night shadows gather around the house.

In the window the lamp is lit for Mother and Father.

Down in the sandbox the pail and the shovel
are left by the castle door.

The goldfish play with the moonfish deep in the
lily pool.

Those old frogs begin to croak. And the fireflies
come from the woods. The giant moth zooms by
looking for the moonflowers.

The warm night-wind tosses our hair. The wind chimes stir. And we all dance, barefooted. Over and over the grass! We play tag in and out. With the wind and with each other.

We climb the tree just to be in a tree at night.

And we make a little camp and pretend we're on an island for the night.

We make up songs. And poems. And we turn somersaults all over the grass.

We tell ghost stories. And holler "Boo!" under the window.

We jump and jump, over and over, and higher and higher. But nobody ever has touched the moon.

We run and run around the house. And the balloon of a moon grows and grows.

A GIANT shadow comes! We hide! Bigger and bigger he comes across the lawn! It's coming! The GIANT!

He lights his pipe — and he LAUGHS! Father is the giant taking a walk to look at his roses.

Mother calls from the door, "Children, oh children." But we're not children, we're the Moon Jumpers!

"It's time," she says.

"Good night, Moon."

The bed is white and cool and the pillow as soft as the night.

The moon sails on up the sky. And we fall asleep
and dream of tomorrow's sun.